Curious George Joins the Team

Written by Cynthia Platt

Illustrated in the style of H. A. Rey by Mary O'Keefe Young

HOUGHTON MIFFLIN HARCOURT
Boston   New York

To Megan, John, and Ellie—good friends indeed.

—C.P.

For Hal, my MVP.

—M.O'.K.Y.

www.hmhco.com

The illustrations in this book were done in watercolor and black colored pencil.
The text type was set in Garamond.

IBSN 978-0-544-46500-8

Manufactured in China
SCP 10 9 8 7 6 5 4 3 2
4500593668

This is George.
George is a good little monkey
and always very curious.

This morning, George had a playdate at a brand-new playground.
George loves playgrounds. And anything new is always exciting!

George was going to meet his new friend, Tina, at the playground. "You're going to love this park, George," the man with the yellow hat told him.

"There's a basketball court and a special play structure that was built so that children with or without disabilities can all play together."

George tried to imagine what this special playground might look like as they drove there.

When George and his friend pulled into the playground, the park looked even better than he had dreamed!

There was a giant castle in the middle with wide ramps
to run up and down. There were special swings—some
that had great comfy seats, and one that could fit a
wheelchair. George saw Tina on a swing!

As the man with the yellow hat talked to Tina's grandmother, George studied the play structure. Could he do everything in this new playground in just one day? He thought so . . .

He ran up a ramp just as Tina sped up behind
him. George loved the way Tina raced around the
play structure on four wheels. She was amazing!

First he climbed the monkey bars. He was very good at this!

Then Tina zoomed down a cool wide slide. She was very good at that.

Next, they played tic-tac-toe. They were both very good at tic-tac-toe!

The sound of a ball bouncing distracted George. There was a group of kids throwing an orange ball into a hoop. George and Tina raced over to watch them.

Tina was very excited.

"I love to play basketball!" she said.
Her grandmother came over.

"Why don't you ask if you can
join?" she said. But Tina was too shy
to ask, and she looked a little sad.

George tried to cheer her up. He jumped as high as he could and swung all around the trees over her head. Tina laughed as she watched him. The kids on the basketball court stopped to watch too.

"I'm Jenna. And we're the Slam Dunkers," a girl told George. "Do you want to come and play with our team?"

He had never played basketball before. He was so curious, he forgot he was playing with Tina. He ran off onto the court and took the ball.

Basketball was so much fun!
George learned to dribble
the ball and throw it to his
teammates.

He was super at jump-
ing up to catch the ball
when it rebounded off
the backboard.

During a break Tina wheeled her chair onto the basketball court. "Can I play too?" she asked in a quiet voice. George hoped they'd be on the same team!

But the other kids weren't so sure.
"You play basketball?" Jenna asked.
"Sure, I play all the time," answered Tina.

Then George had an idea. He got
the ball, and with one quick leap,
he threw it to Tina!

Tina looked surprised,
but then she wheeled
onto the court. She
shot—and she scored!

All of the kids on the Slam Dunkers cheered, while George turned flips of joy.

Then Jenna threw the ball to Tina— and she scored again.

Tina was a great basketball player!

"Like I said, I play a lot at home," she reminded them.

"I can tell," said Jenna. "We play every week. Do you and George want to join our team?"

George and Tina played basketball all afternoon. They even made plans to come and play together another day soon. Tina and George were part of the team now, and they always scored the most baskets!

FEB   2019